TOPSY-TURVY TRACY

The Grimy-Slimy Bug Safari

written by Susie Taylor

illustrated by Tammie Lyon

Zonderkidz

Zonder**kidz**®

The children's group of Zondervan

www.zonderkidz.com

Topsy-Turvy Tracy: The Grimy-Slimy Bug Safari
Copyright © 2004 by Susie Taylor
Illustrations copyright © 2004 by Tammie Lyon

Requests for information should be addressed to:
Zonderkidz, Grand Rapids, Michigan 49530

Library of Congress Cataloging-in-Publication Data

Taylor, Susie, 1963–
    The grimy–slimy bug safari / Susie Taylor. –1st. ed.
       p. cm.
    Summary: Tracy climbs up a tree while looking for some bugs and winds
up seeing God's creatures upside-down,
    ISBN 0-310-70443-X (Hardcover)
    [1. Insects—Fiction. 2. Christian life—Fiction.
3. Stories in rhyme.] I. Title.
PZ8.3.T2183Gr 2003
dc22   2003018704

Zonderkidz is a trademark of Zondervan.

Editor: Gwen Ellis
Art Direction and interior design: Michelle Lenger

Printed in China

04 05 06 07/HK/4 3 2 1

For Lindsay and Ryan,
my explorers!
—s.t.k.

For Lee, who moved me out to the country
which has given me endless things to explore.
—t.l.

Tracy was a little girl
No bigger than a minute,
And each day she explored God's world
And all the things within it!

On the night that was before today,
She had a plan in mind
To venture out and search the yard
For bugs of every kind.

Big bugs, small bugs,
And ones with lots of feet,
Even grimy, slimy bugs,
The kind frogs like to eat!

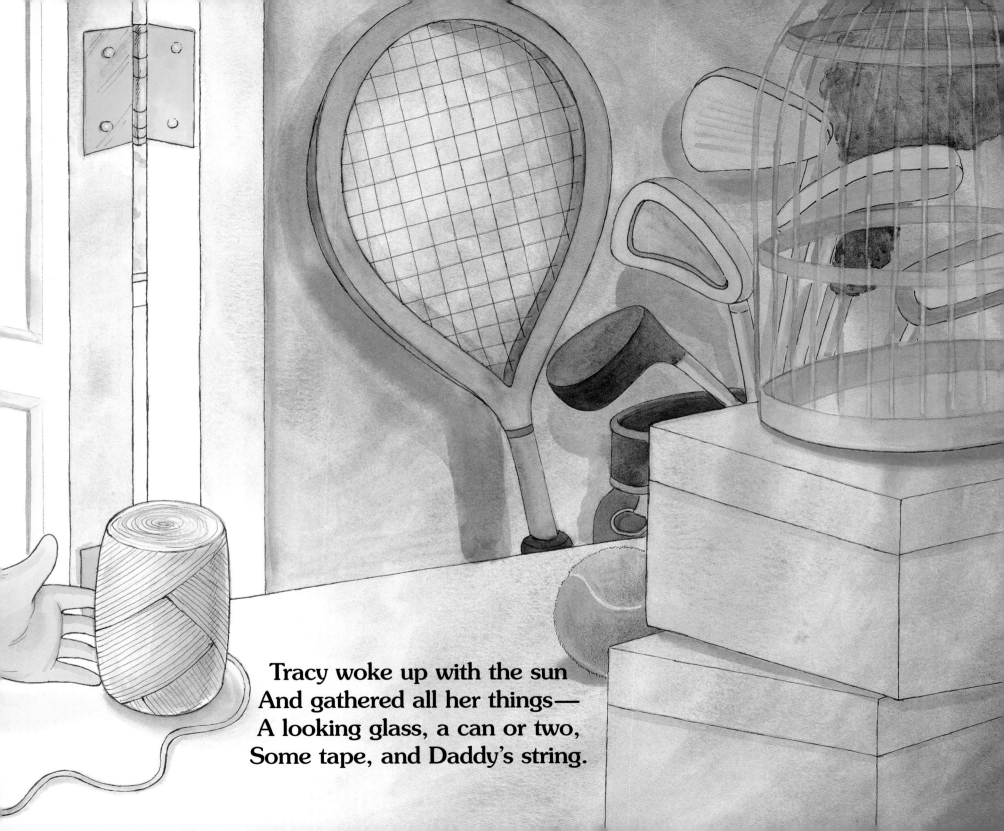

Tracy woke up with the sun
And gathered all her things—
A looking glass, a can or two,
Some tape, and Daddy's string.

She saw a shiny bright blue bug
Just hanging on a tree,
And longing for a closer look,
She shimmied up to see!

And as she made her way back down,
Her sneaker lace got caught.
It wrapped around a little branch.
"I'm very stuck," she thought.

So stuck was Tracy in that tree
That when she moved around,
No longer was she right side up
But swinging upside down!

Now, Tracy liked it upside down,
It made for lots of fun.
A great adventure was in store;
Her bug hunt had begun!

While hanging upside down
From that big branch upon the tree,
Tracy saw a ladybug,
A butterfly, a bee.

Flip and see what Tracy saw!

"This being stuck is not so bad,"
Thought Tracy with two shrugs.
"I'll just use my problem now
And hunt for lots of bugs!"

Flip and see what Tracy saw!

All creatures that are made by God
Are special and unique!
Whether right side up or upside down,
They all deserve a peek!

Flip and see what Tracy saw!

While as an upside–downer,
Tracy saw a slimy snail.

Then she noticed two
small spiders
Traveling down their
webby trail.

A pill bug wandered up the tree,
Or was it going down?
When Tracy tried to grab it,
It rolled up and hit the ground!

Then tucked away behind a leaf,
A caterpillar's cocoon
Was caring for a butterfly
Who'd fly out very soon!

Then Tracy heard a grumble
From her tummy upside down,
For the breakfast she had eaten
Was getting shaken all around.

So, she loosened up her shoelace
And pulled her sneaker free,
Then swung around to right side up
And jumped down from the tree.

Back on the ground, she turned around
And found her bug-hunt things,
Searching, now, for crawly bugs
Or maybe one with wings.

It is much better hunting bugs
Upon the solid ground,
Watching all God's wonders
Right side up or upside down!